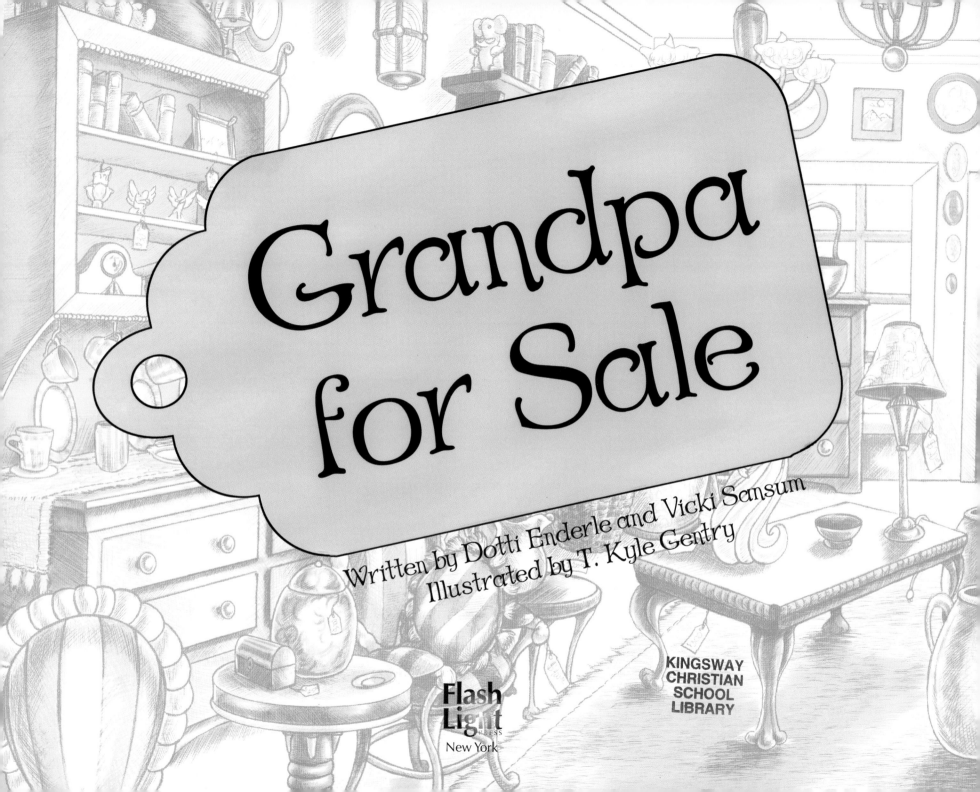

Grandpa for Sale

Written by Dotti Enderle and Vicki Sansum
Illustrated by T. Kyle Gentry

Flash Light PRESS
New York

For all the authors who've inspired me. —DE
To my parents, who encouraged me to read and to imagine. —VS
To my parents, Ray and Brenda, and to my wife, Katie,
who all helped me get here. —TKG

Copyright © 2007 by Flashlight Press
Text copyright © 2007 by Dotti Enderle and Vicki Sansum
Illustrations copyright © 2007 by T. Kyle Gentry
All rights reserved, including the right of reproduction,
in whole or in part, in any form. Printed at Hemed Press, Israel.
First Edition — April 2007

Library of Congress Control Number: 2006937223
ISBN-13 9780972922586
ISBN-10 097292258X

Editor: Shari Dash Greenspan
Graphic Design: The Virtual Paintbrush
This book was typeset in Old Paris Nouveau.
Illustrations were rendered in traditional graphite pencil
and digital pencil, watercolor, and chalk.

Distributed by Independent Publishers Group

Flashlight Press · 3709 13th Avenue · Brooklyn, NY 11218
www.FlashlightPress.com

At Oldman's Antiques, Lizzie dusted the lamps, the books, the clocks, and the spindly tables. She even dusted the bald spot on Grandpa's head as he snoozed on a Louis XVI settee.

The tiny bell over the door tinkled as a woman breezed in. Her pink stole and suit matched the miniature poodle in her arms. Lizzie had never seen anyone with hair so tall!

The woman peered at Lizzie through rhinestone glasses. "You seem quite young to be running such an establishment."

"I'm watching the store until my mother comes back," Lizzie said. After all, she was quite capable of running such an establishment – for ten minutes anyway.

"I'm Mrs. Bradley Larchmont the Third, and this is Giselle." The dog yapped at the sound of her name. "If you don't mind, I'd like to browse."

Lizzie certainly didn't mind. That's all anyone ever did in Oldman's Antiques.

Mrs. Larchmont inspected each item with a gloved hand. "I'll take this," she said, tossing Lizzie a fringed silk pillow,

"and this," handing her a vase,

"and I simply can't live without this," stacking on
a lamp.

Then she glanced down at the Louis XVI settee.
"Oh, my stars! Look at this! I don't think I've ever
seen one for sale. How much?"

Lizzie checked the price tag. "Five hundred dollars."

"What a bargain!" the woman said. "Does he come with a set of teeth?"

"Teeth?" Lizzie asked.

"Yes. He's not wearing any."

Lizzie gawked at Mrs. Larchmont and her pink pooch. "The settee?" Lizzie asked.

"No," said the woman, scratching the tiny poodle's chin. "I have a dozen of those at home already. How much for *this* charming antique?"

"But he's my grandpa!" Lizzie protested.

"In that case, you must know how much he's worth." Mrs. Larchmont tapped her foot impatiently and Giselle wagged her tail.

Lizzie looked nervously at Grandpa. "But he's not for sale," she explained.

"Nonsense, my dear. Everyone has a price.
I'll give you five hundred dollars for him."
"Five hundred dollars?" Lizzie repeated.

For five hundred dollars,
Lizzie could buy the treehouse
she'd always wanted. She could start her own
club and be President. She'd be the most
popular girl in the neighborhood.

But what good would a treehouse be without Grandpa there to help her build it?

President Lizzie's Tree House

"Okay," Mrs. Larchmont said,
sucking in a breath. "One thousand."

One thousand dollars! With that much money Lizzie could
buy a small boat and sail out on the lake any time she wanted.
She could lie back and float lazily along, or look for the
mysterious monster that lurked on the bottom.

But what good would a boat be
without Grandpa there to
steer and fish and sing
sailor songs?

Mrs. Larchmont lifted one thin eyebrow. Giselle lifted her ears. "So you want to bargain, do you? Very well. Five thousand dollars."

Lizzie pictured herself in her very own Lavender Dream Bedroom Set. The lace curtains would match the ruffled canopy on the bed, and she'd have her very own dressing table. To sleep in that room would be like dreaming on a fluffy marshmallow.

But what good would a fancy bedroom be without
Grandpa there to tuck her in and tell her bedtime stories?

"No deal," Lizzie said.

Mrs. Larchmont adjusted the sparkly glasses on her pointy nose. "Ten thousand."

Ten thousand dollars!
Wouldn't that buy an
entire ice cream shop
with every frozen
flavor ever invented?
And sprinkles?
And chocolate chips?
And hot fudge!
She could have an
ice cream shop with
lots of customers
who'd actually buy
something! Selling
ice cream would
certainly be more fun
than dusting antiques.

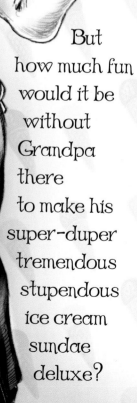

FLAVORS
Yummy Yo-Yo Yogurt
Rip Roaring Ripple Su...
Peachy Keen Crea...
Delicious Banana Ra... S...
Choca-laka Hula...
Fudge M... M...
Rock...Roll Rocky Ro...

But how much fun would it be without Grandpa there to make his super-duper tremendous stupendous ice cream sundae deluxe?

Mrs. Larchmont gritted her teeth. Giselle softly growled. They leaned in, face to face with Lizzie. "Fifty...thousand...dollars, and that's my final offer."

Lizzie's
knees wobbled.
She felt woozy.
With that much money
she could build an
amusement park with the
loopiest roller coaster ever,
and her friends could ride for free
anytime they wanted. Lizzie dwelled
on this vision for a full minute.

SCREAMING MOUNTAIN

But what good
would an amusement park be
without Grandpa there
to scream the loudest?

Lizzie took a deep breath and leaned in too. "Mrs. Larchmont," she announced, "not everyone has a price, and not everything is for sale."

Mrs. Larchmont stamped her foot. "Well, if I can't buy everything I want, then I won't buy anything at all!" And she swept out the door in a furious huff.

Lizzie kissed Grandpa gently, then walked over to the cash register. Smiling, she pushed the big red button...

Ding! NO SALE!